A GRAIN OF RICE

HELENA CLARE PITTMAN

DELACORTE PRESS

All rights reserved. Published in the United States by Delacorte Press, an imprint of Random House Children's Books, a division of Penguin Random House LLC, New York. Originally published in hardcover by Hastings House, New York, New York, in 1986, and in paperback in the United States by Yearling, an imprint of Random House Children's Books, New York, in 1995.

Delacorte Press is a registered trademark and the colophon is a trademark of Penguin Random House LLC.

Visit us on the Web! rhcbooks.com

Educators and librarians, for a variety of teaching tools, visit us at RHTeachersLibrarians.com

Library of Congress Cataloging-in-Publication Data is available upon request.
ISBN 978-1-5247-6552-1 (hc)
ISBN 978-1-5247-6553-8 (ebook)

The text of this book is set in 15.5-point Warnock Pro Light.

Printed in the United States of America
10 9 8 7 6 5 4 3 2 1
First Edition

To my parents,
Florence and Jack Steinberg,
my sister, Jolene, and
my children, Theo and Galen

Once a year the Emperor of China opened his court so that even the humblest of his people could come before him. It was on one such day that Pong Lo, the son of a farmer, knelt at the Emperor's feet.

"Imperial Majesty," said Pong Lo, "I have come to ask for your daughter's hand in marriage."

The Emperor's lords were shocked.

The Princess Chang Wu, who stood near her father's throne, lowered her eyes and blushed.

"How dare you make such a request?" demanded the Emperor. His eyes were fierce and his long mustache twitched. The peasant pressed his forehead to the silken carpet.

"Forgive me, Your Majesty . . . ," he mumbled.

"Speak up!" commanded the Emperor.

Pong Lo lifted his head. ". . . but I am more than qualified to be her husband!" he declared.

The lords giggled.

"Qualified!" cried the outraged Emperor, gripping his sword. "Such boldness qualifies you to lose your head!"

"But it is my head which qualifies me!" replied Pong Lo. "It is wise and quick and more than a little clever, and would make me as fine a prince as China has ever seen."

"Prince!" shrieked the Emperor. "A peasant cannot be a prince! A prince must come from noble blood!" His mustache twitched madly.

"My blood may not be noble, Your

Majesty," returned Pong Lo, "but it, too, is clever."

"What do you mean?" the Emperor demanded.

"Though it has to find its way through seventy thousand miles of veins," answered the peasant quietly, "it never fails to reach my heart."

Now the lords smiled behind their fans at Pong Lo's skillful answer. Princess Chang Wu's black eyes sparkled.

"Enough of this!" growled the Emperor, raising his sword.

"Father, wait!" The scent of lotus

blossoms filled the air as the Princess rushed to the Emperor's side. "Don't be hasty, Father," she begged. "The young man is clever. He could be useful!"

"He will be useful when his clever tongue is no longer flapping in his head!" the Emperor snapped.

"Father," the Princess coaxed, "since he is so good with numbers, perhaps he can work in the storeroom."

The Emperor eyed the peasant shrewdly. Pong Lo's head was once again pressed to the floor. He looked so humble.

The Princess smiled hopefully at her father and placed her hand gently upon his. Her touch was like the brush of silk stirring in a summer breeze. Suddenly the Emperor's cares felt lighter.

Sighing, the Emperor sat down again. "My gentle daughter," he said, looking fondly at Chang Wu, "for your sake I will spare him. But he will have to prove his worth. He can scrub the storeroom. If he works hard he can stay."

So Pong Lo was given a place to sleep in the farthest corner of the palace, and he was put to work. He cleaned the deep wooden storeroom shelves. He washed the grain bins and scrubbed the stone floor, and polished it carefully with a wax he made himself. It gleamed as it never had before.

"How do you do that?" asked the Imperial Storeroom Keeper.

"Just an old family recipe," Pong Lo answered cheerfully. And when he had finished that, instead of going off to drink tea or sit under a tree, he helped the other storeroom servants, sorting the grains that came from the Emperor's fields. The expression on his face

was always pleasant, and his step was light. As he worked he often hummed a merry tune which was so delightful that the other servants couldn't help but sing with him.

Pong Lo did everything so well that the Imperial Storeroom Keeper put him in charge of the shelves. He stored the beans and dried fruits. He shelled the nuts and stacked the pickled eggs and vegetables. He laid the teas and spices carefully in their boxes, and kept count of everything. When something was in short supply he always noticed. He knew

where to get even the strangest ingredients and at the best price. He knew so much about rare herbs and spices that before long the Emperor's cooks were seeking his advice.

The Imperial Storeroom Keeper told the Steward. The Steward told the Minister of Palace Affairs. The Minister told the Chamberlain. The Chamberlain told the Prime Minister, and the Prime Minister told the Emperor.

"Hmmm," said the Emperor, stroking his mustache. "Clever indeed! Make him Imperial Assistant to the Imperial Storeroom Keeper.

"Clever is the word!" the servants whispered.

But as if that weren't enough, when his long day in the storeroom ended, Pong Lo asked to help in the kitchen.

At first he sliced and diced and chopped, whistling as he worked. He stirred and sampled, and offered a pleasant suggestion or two. Soon he was salting and seasoning until the fragrance of his sauces steamed through the palace. The Imperial Cooks whistled along with Pong Lo's lively tunes. The Imperial Kitchen Maid trilled a chorus. The waiters stepped jauntily as they carried their trays from the kitchen to the Emperor's table, and everyone from lords to servants looked forward as never before to the next meal—even the Imperial Kitchen Cat, who purred loudly over the leftovers. Pong Lo's recipes were delicious!

The Emperor, who loved to eat, was

delighted. "Excellent!" he remarked to the Princess night after night over dinner. "Make him Imperial Assistant to the Imperial Cook as well!" he told the Prime Minister. Pong Lo was moved to a small room, in keeping with his new position.

Princess Chang Wu listened carefully for any word of Pong Lo. She couldn't forget his handsome face, his cleverness, and his bravery before her father. At every excuse she passed the kitchen or the storeroom to catch a glimpse of him. The smell of the lotus blossoms she wore in her hair followed her, and told Pong Lo that she was near. Then his heartbeat quickened and his song sounded sweeter. Sometimes their eyes met and they shared a smile.

"You have grown so lovely, my dear," said the Emperor to the Princess one day.

"The time is coming to find a husband for you. In the summer I shall invite all the young nobles of China to the palace and I will choose from among them."

The Princess looked sad and hurried away.

As the days passed and summer came, the palace bustled with activity in preparation for the arrival of China's most excellent young noblemen. But Chang Wu seemed not to care. With no hope of marrying Pong Lo, she grew sadder and sadder until at last she only stayed in bed. Her black

eyes lost their sparkle and her cheeks became pale.

The Emperor's physicians shook their heads. Their potions were useless. Day after day the Princess lay with her face to the window. She wouldn't speak or eat. When the Emperor came to sit near her bed, she only wept. Heartsick, the Emperor issued a proclamation: Anyone in China who could cure the Princess would be handsomely rewarded.

Peasants and nobles alike made their way to the royal city. They tried berries and ointments. They tried chants and

spells. Nothing worked. The Princess grew steadily worse.

But late into the night, a light burned in Pong Lo's room. The fragrance of herbs drifted into the corridor as he crushed and pounded and brewed the

leaves and roots he knew so well. One
morning, as the Princess lay dying, he
appeared before the Emperor. His face
was strained from care and lack of sleep
but his gaze was steady.

"Your Majesty," he said, "here is the potion that will cure the Princess Chang Wu." He held out a tiny bottle filled with green liquid.

"How can you be sure?" asked the despairing Emperor.

"The recipe has been in my family for hundreds of years," said Pong Lo. "It will cure the disease if the heart is willing. But you must tell the Princess that it comes from me."

"If she lives you shall have anything you want!" cried the Emperor, and clutching the bottle, he hurried to the Princess' bed.

Chang Wu opened her eyes and looked at her father with a sad smile. A tear fell to her pillow like a petal from a fading blossom. The Emperor thought his heart would break.

"Take this, my child," he said. "It comes from Pong Lo."

"Pong Lo!" exclaimed the Princess with a weak cry. A flush came over her pale face.

"My precious one," said the Emperor

sadly. "If it makes you well, I will grant him anything he asks."

"Will you, Father?" cried the Princess. "Will you really?" And without another word she drank down Pong Lo's potion.

The next morning the palace was alive with the news: the Princess had eaten breakfast! By the following afternoon she was sitting in a chair by the window. Overcome with joy and relief, the Emperor called his lords together to celebrate with him in his court, and he summoned Pong Lo.

"Honorable Pong Lo,"
he said. "I owe my hap-
piness to you. Name the
reward and it shall be
yours."

"There is only one
thing I have ever desired,
Your Majesty," said Pong
Lo, "and that is the hand
of the Princess Chang
Wu."

The Emperor's smile
vanished and he looked
troubled. "Good Pong

Lo," he said. "I am saddened by your request, for you have more than proven your worth. But still I cannot grant the Princess's hand to a humble peasant. There must be something else that will satisfy you."

Pong Lo lowered his eyes sadly. "That is not possible, Your Majesty," he said quietly, and for a long moment he seemed to be thinking. "But perhaps there *is* something else," he said at last.

"Anything!" cried the Emperor.

"A grain of rice," said the peasant.

"A grain of rice?" repeated the

Emperor. He glanced at his lords, but they had long since stopped laughing at Pong Lo. The Emperor lowered his voice and leaned forward. "Surely there must be something more?"

"No, Your Majesty," said Pong Lo.

"That's nonsense!" exclaimed the Emperor. "Ask me for fine silks, the grandest room in the palace, a stable full of stallions—they shall be yours!"

"If I cannot marry the Princess, then one grain of rice is all I desire."

"That is preposterous," said the

Emperor. "Take a chest of gold. A herd of oxen!"

"A grain of rice," said Pong Lo.

"A servant of your own!" cried the Emperor.

"A grain of rice will do," said Pong Lo. "But if His Majesty insists, he may double the amount every day for a hundred days."

"It is ridiculous!" scoffed the Emperor, twisting his mustache between his fingers and eying Pong Lo. "But it is granted."

That very afternoon a grain of rice

was delivered to Pong Lo's room. It rested on a tiny cushion, in the center of a silver bird's nest. If the peasant insisted on being humble, the Emperor could at least be generous.

With Princess Chang Wu's health improving every day, life in the palace returned to normal. Pong Lo went back to his work in the kitchen.

On the second day a fine china cup, painted with delicate pink flowers, was left at Pong Lo's door. Two grains of rice had been placed inside.

On the third day, four grains were left, resting neatly on the back of an alabaster swan. Pong Lo picked it up on his way back from the kitchen and put it in the corner of his room—next to the silver bird's nest and the fine china cup.

On the fourth day, eight grains of rice were left in an enameled bowl. Pong Lo admired its simple beauty.

On the fifth day, sixteen grains arrived on a golden plate.

Thirty-two grains of rice were

brought on the sixth day, nestled delicately in the mouth of a carved dragonfish. The corner of Pong Lo's room was getting cluttered.

Sixty-four grains, resting in a small boat made of precious stones, appeared on the seventh day.

On the eighth, a jade box arrived. It held one hundred and twenty-eight grains of rice.

Two hundred and fifty-six grains of rice were delivered on the ninth day. They lay on an ivory tray.

"Hmmm," remarked the Emperor on the tenth day. "Five hundred and twelve grains of rice! It will be more than a thousand tomorrow!"

By the twelfth day the grains of rice numbered two thousand and forty-eight. They were sent to Pong Lo in a box covered with embroidered silk. Pong Lo's room was crowded with gold and jewels and ivory and alabaster, and littered with grains of rice. There was hardly room left for Pong Lo. The Emperor had him moved to a small house on the palace grounds.

On the eighteenth day two oxen arrived at the new house. Each carried two ebony chests. One hundred thirty-one thousand and seventy-two grains of rice were in the chests.

"Five hundred twenty-four thousand,

two hundred and eighty-eight grains of rice!" exclaimed the Emperor on the twentieth day. "Tomorrow it will be more than a million!" His anxious fingers

pulled at his mustache and he summoned the Imperial Mathematician.

The mathematician pushed and pulled at the ebony beads of his abacus and he scribbled with his brush on a paper scroll. "Imperial Majesty, at this rate, in ten days there will be no rice left in the palace!"

The emperor paced and thought. "Then we shall have to get more!"

On the twenty-fifth day, sixteen million, seven hundred seventy-seven thousand, two hundred and sixteen grains of rice were delivered in brocaded sacks,

carried on the backs of twenty-five of
the Emperor's Imperial Horses. On the
twenty-sixth day the Emperor issued a
proclamation: for every bushel of rice

brought to the palace he would pay one piece of gold. Rice poured in from all over China.

Pong Lo grew richer every day, and

the Emperor grew more anxious. How could this go on for a hundred days! Again he summoned his mathematician. The mathematician's fingers flew and the abacus beads clacked.

"Your Majesty!" he cried. "By next

month that young man will own all the rice in China!"

The Emperor was beside himself. But he had given his word before his Court. "Then we shall have to get more!"

Five hundred thirty-six million, eight hundred and seventy thousand, nine hundred and twelve grains of rice were delivered to Pong Lo on the thirtieth day. It took forty servants to carry them in huge brass urns.

By the thirty-fifth day it was clear that Pong Lo would have to move again. The Emperor gave him his summer palace.

Ships were sent across the ocean to buy more rice. Every day new servants had to be found. From morning until night they counted out grains of rice. The matter of Princess Chang Wu's marriage was postponed indefinitely.

On the fortieth day, a caravan of one hundred elephants was sent to the summer palace. On their backs were

loaded great trunks carved of rosewood
and inlaid with mother-of-pearl. All together they held five hundred forty-nine

billion, seven hundred fifty-five million, eight hundred thirteen thousand, eight hundred and eighty-eight grains of rice!

The Emperor watched the procession gloomily from his balcony. The mathematician worked his abacus, sitting in a tangle of scrolls at the Emperor's feet. He scribbled and muttered while the beads of the abacus clicked and clacked.

"My figures must be wrong!" he shouted at last. "There couldn't be that much rice in the world!" So he started his calculations again. He stammered and swore and spluttered and broke his brushes and tore up paper and grew more and more frustrated until finally the Emperor had to send him away.

Alone in his private chamber, the Emperor sat with his head in his hands. Soon his treasury would be empty.

He called his lords to his Court. And he summoned Pong Lo.

The young man arrived at the palace dressed richly in the clothes he had bought with his rice. Twenty servants of his own attended him. His step was light and the expression on his face was

as good-natured as ever. He bowed to
the Emperor and smiled at the Princess,
who stood in her place at the Emperor's
side. Chang Wu's eyes sparkled as she
returned Pong Lo's smile.

"Greetings, most honorable Pong
Lo," the Emperor began. "You are looking well. It has been some time since we
have met."

"Thank you, Your Majesty," said Pong

Lo. "To be precise, it has been forty days."

"Only forty days," lamented the Emperor. "Life at the summer palace is pleasant, I hope?"

"The view is wonderful," returned Pong Lo. "And my days are filled with activity. Counting, storing, selling rice—"

"Yes!" the Emperor interrupted. "They must be. I imagine you are growing tired of rice?" he asked hopefully.

"Oh no, Your Majesty," said Pong Lo. "It will make a fine barrier against the winter wind. And there are so many things to be made with it. Rice paper,

rice wine, rice cakes, rice noodles, rice syrup—I could go on and on."

The Emperor looked gloomy. "I do not doubt it," he said. "Things have not gone as well for me, however. I have been having a problem with my daughter, Chang Wu. The mere mention of marriage sends her into a fit of melancholy."

The Princess blushed.

The Emperor shifted uncomfortably on his throne. "Honorable Pong Lo," he began again, "you have become a rich man."

Pong Lo smiled modestly.

"Richer than any nobleman in China," said the Emperor. "At last you can care for my daughter as a Princess should be cared for. I have therefore decided to make you a Prince and grant you her hand in marriage." Here the Emperor leaned forward and lowered his voice. "But no more rice!" he said.

The clever Pong Lo bowed again. "I humbly accept your offer, Father," he said.

A sigh went through the Court. "When is dinner?" someone whispered.

Pong Lo and Chang Wu were

married. The wedding feast was wonderful, its preparation supervised by the new Prince himself. There was bean soup, and bean curd. Bean paste

and sprouted beans. Pressed duck and
steamed dumplings. Fish with millet
and pheasant with millet. There were
barley cakes and barley candies. Wheat

noodles, potato noodles, corn noodles, fried noodles. But—out of respect for the Emperor's feelings—there was not a single grain of rice.

The Emperor lived to be an old man. At his death, Prince Pong Lo and Princess Chang Wu inherited his kingdom. They lived happily, and ruled wisely, all their days.

THE MATH BEHIND THE STORY

A Grain of Rice is a beautifully told tale about love, ingenuity ... and math! In this story, we learn how young Pong Lo uses a little mathematical thinking to win over Princess Chang Wu's father, the Emperor. Pong Lo tries all kinds of things to impress the Emperor, but it's not until he uses his smarts to make numbers—and the amount of rice he owns—grow quickly that he gains the Emperor's respect and builds a fortune!

While I can't guarantee that being clever with numbers is a surefire path to marrying a prince or princess, I can assure you that being comfortable with numbers, seeing patterns in them, and learning to understand equations will pay off someday. It might be in the quality of your work, or it might be in the fun and satisfaction of understanding something interesting. That something might involve money, but it might also involve science and other real-world phenomena. Math is everywhere.

Now, back to Pong Lo. Pong Lo starts by asking the Emperor for a single grain of rice, but then—after a little encouragement—further asks that the Emperor "double the amount every day" for him, for one hundred days. It doesn't sound like a large request to the Emperor, so he agrees.

Would you have agreed? Quick: imagine holding a grain of rice in your hand. It might not look like much, but in just forty days the Emperor is forced to deliver more than five hundred *billion* grains of rice on the backs of one hundred elephants! (I did some checking, and that's about twenty thousand tons of rice! For comparison, your car weighs around two tons, so this is the weight of roughly ten thousand cars.) Faced with the idea of doubling the amount of rice again the next day, the Emperor realizes he can't keep his promise to Pong Lo. He

simply cannot deliver that much rice. As quickly as the rice accumulates, the poor Emperor's good mood disintegrates.

Is it hard to picture that much rice? Let's make the point another way. Suppose that this doubling rule were instead a rule about your height and how you grow. Say that in the first year of your life, you are just an inch tall, but then each year you grow twice as many inches as the year before. You might say, "No way! I don't want to be tiny my whole life!" But what does doubling do? In the second year of your life, you grow two inches, and in the third year, four more. In the tenth year of your life, you will grow—get ready for this—512 inches. That is more than 42 feet! It's 42 feet and 8 inches, to be exact, which is taller than a school bus is long! You'll definitely make your school basketball team if you grow like that. Whether with grains of rice or inches per year, you can see that the numbers may start small, but they get big very quickly once you start doubling them.

Another way to look at this progression is with a table. Here is a table that shows how Pong Lo accumulates grains of rice over the first ten days:

Day	Grains of Rice
1	1
2	2
3	4
4	8
5	16
6	32
7	64
8	128
9	256
10	512

A list of numbers is fine, but a picture's worth a thousand words, as they say, so to the right, we show the growth using a graph.

In this picture, going from left to right, we mark off the days from 1 to 10. Going from bottom to top, we mark off the number of grains of rice that Pong Lo receives from 0 to 600. Since the numbers going from bottom to top have a wide range, we don't have space to make a mark for each number. If you look closely, you will see that we've divided each section of 100 grains into

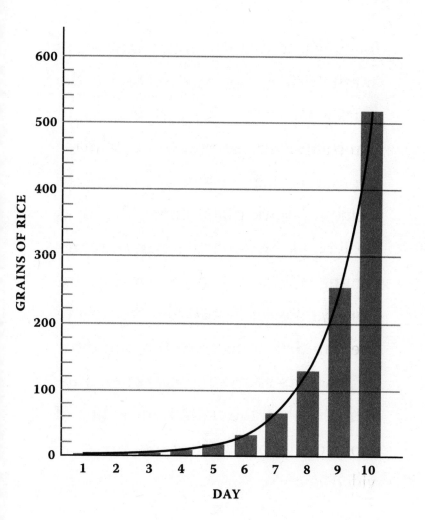

5 chunks, so that each mark represents another 20 grains of rice. Above the marker for each day, we draw a bar in the graph that is level with the number of grains of rice received on that day. For example, above 10, the top of the bar is positioned between the marks representing 500 and 520. If you had a microscope and a ruler, you would be able to confirm that, in fact, the top of the bar is 512 units above the line on the bottom, equal to the number of grains of rice received on day 10.

The takeaway from this picture is how quickly the curve connecting the tops of the bars swoops up as the numbers increase. And it gets even steeper as you go out farther and the number of days increases. Between days 9 and 10, the number of grains received increases by 256. Between days 10 and 11, by 512, and so on. From 1 grain to over 500 billion over the course of just 40 days—that is extraordinarily fast growth.

What do we call this kind of growth? We could call it "really fast growth,"

or perhaps something more precise like "growth by doubling." But this fast growth has a special name: "exponential growth." The term exponential growth has to do with the mathematical operation we use to calculate the number of grains on any given day: the process of "exponentiation." (Don't worry. I'll explain!)

Exponentiation is another way of

saying "using powers." Have you learned about powers yet? Well, you might have, but maybe under different names. Have you been introduced to the idea of squaring a number? That's the operation of multiplying a number by itself. 1 squared is 1 x 1, which equals 1. 2 squared is 2 x 2, which equals 4. 3 squared is 3 x 3, which equals 9, and so on. (Quick: What is 4 squared?) The reason we call it "squaring" is because the area of a square is equal to the number you get when you multiply the length of one side of the square by itself. For example, if you have a square with sides that are a length of 2 (and it could be 2 of anything: feet, meters, yards, etc.), then the area of that square would be 2 x 2 = 4 (square feet, square meters, square yards, etc.).

You could also multiply a number by itself three times! This is called "cubing." 1 cubed is 1 x 1 x 1, which equals 1. 2 cubed is 2 x 2 x 2, which equals 8. 3 cubed is 3 x 3 x 3, which equals 27. And so on. Can you guess why we call it cubing? That's right! It has to do with the volume of a cube. The volume of a cube is equal to the number you get when you multiply the length of one side by itself three times.

Why stop there? We could also multiply a number by itself four times or five times (or any number of times), but we don't have good names for those specific operations. Instead, we say that we are "raising a number to the fourth power" if we multiply it by itself four times, or "raising it to the fifth power" if we multiply it by itself five times.

In other words, a "power" refers to how many times you multiply a number by itself. Squaring a number is called "raising it to the second power," cubing is "raising a number to the third power," and so on. By that definition, "2 to the second power" is 2 x 2, or 4, "2 to the third power" is 2 x 2 x 2, or 8, and "2 to the fourth power" is 2 x 2 x 2 x 2, or 16. Also, for that matter, "2 to the first power" is 2. (It's even possible to make sense of "2 raised to the zero power!" But we won't go there now. . . .)

Now we're finally reaching the end of our explanation, because when we raise 2 (or any number) to a power, that power is called the exponent, and we write it like this:

$2^1 = 2$

$2^2 = 2 \times 2 = 4$

$2^3 = 2 \times 2 \times 2 = 4 \times 2 = 8$

$2^4 = 2 \times 2 \times 2 \times 2 = 4 \times 2 \times 2 = 8 \times 2 = 16$

Because 2 is always the "base" in these equations, and only the powers change, these equations all represent different "powers of 2." This is just a term that means 2 has been raised to a certain power. "Powers of 3" would look the same, except you would have 3 as your base number instead of 2:

$$3^1 = 3$$
$$3^2 = 3 \times 3 = 9$$
$$3^3 = 3 \times 3 \times 3 = 9 \times 3 = 27$$
$$3^4 = 3 \times 3 \times 3 \times 3 = 9 \times 3 \times 3 = 27 \times 3 = 81$$

To connect this all back to Pong Lo's story, the amount of rice he receives each day can always be expressed as a power of 2, because it is always multiplied by 2 (or doubled) from the day before. On day 1, he gets one grain of rice. On day 2, he gets two grains of rice, which is $2^1 = 2$. On day 3, he gets $2^2 = 2 \times 2 = 4$ grains of rice. On day 4, he gets $2^3 = 2 \times 2 \times 2 = 8$, and so forth. Because the exponent increases by one each day as the rice doubles, we call the pattern of growth exponential growth.

On day 40, when the Emperor gives up, the number of grains of rice he has to come up with is 2^{39} grains! This might not look significant, but there is a lot of power (get it? "power!") packed into this notation:

$$2^{39} = 2 \times 2 \times 2 \times 2 \times 2 \times 2 \times 2 \times 2 \times 2 \times 2 \times 2 \times$$
$$2 \times 2 \times 2 \times 2 \times 2 \times 2 \times 2 \times 2 \times 2 \times 2 \times 2 \times 2 \times$$
$$2 \times 2 \times 2 \times 2 \times 2 \times 2 \times 2 \times 2 \times 2 \times 2 \times 2 \times 2 \times$$
$$2 \times 2 \times 2 \times 2 = 549{,}755{,}813{,}888$$

I can't even fit it on one line! And now we know that 2^{39} is over 500 billion!

You still with me? I hope so! Give yourself a pat on the back for making it this far. In fact, if you want to stop reading now, that's completely fine. You've already learned some pretty interesting stuff (and read at least one or two bad math puns). But if you want to learn something even more advanced, keep reading!

*

Like so many things in math, the closer you look, the more there is to discover. What we've seen is just the beginning of the fascinating properties of exponents. I'm hoping you might be interested enough to join me on one extra observation, now that you are a master of powers of two. It's about another pattern we can see if we take a moment to look at how much total rice Pong Lo has received by the end of each day.

Let's assume that Pong Lo never parts with any of his rice as he receives it. How much rice does he have in total at the end of every day? That's easy to figure out using the numbers we've already calculated for each day's rice delivery. We just add them up! Here are the totals at the end of each of the first ten days:

Day	Rice Grains Delivered	Total Rice Grains
1	1	1
2	2	3
3	4	7
4	8	15
5	16	31
6	32	63
7	64	127
8	128	255
9	256	511
10	512	1023

Hmm . . . notice anything? Each day,
the total number of grains of rice that

Pong Lo has (assuming he didn't give any away or sell any) is exactly one less than the number he will receive on the next day! If we write this as a collection of equations, we see the following:

Total on Day 1	= 1		= 2 - 1
Total on Day 2	= 1 + 2		= 4 - 1
Total on Day 3	= 1 + 2 + 4		= 8 - 1
Total on Day 4	= 1 + 2 + 4 + 8		= 16 - 1

Now let's rewrite these using powers of two:

Total on Day 1 $= 1$ $= 2^1 - 1$

Total on Day 2 $= 1 + 2^1$ $= 2^2 - 1$

Total on Day 3 $= 1 + 2^1 + 2^2$ $= 2^3 - 1$

Total on Day 4 $= 1 + 2^1 + 2^2 + 2^3 = 2^4 - 1$

This is the beginning of a wonderful pattern possessed by powers of 2! If you use it to find the total on day 5, you will see that it still holds. In fact, it holds for any day that you have the patience to investigate.

The powers of 2 have all sorts of amazing properties and patterns, and with this little introduction we've seen what is just the first grain of rice in the vast and beautiful world of mathematics, full of mysteries, surprises, and most of all . . . fun.

—Daniel Rockmore,
Professor of Mathematics
and Computer Science,
Dartmouth College

ABOUT THE AUTHOR-ILLUSTRATOR

HELENA CLARE PITTMAN is the author of numerous books for children, including the acclaimed *A Grain of Rice*, *The Snowman's Path*, *The Angel Tree*, and *Once When I Was Scared*.

Visit Helena Clare Pittman at helenaclarepittman.com.